My First
FRENCH
ABC Picture Coloring Book

Deb T. Bunnell

DOVER PUBLICATIONS, INC.
Mineola, New York

Bibliographical Note

My First French ABC Picture Coloring Book is a new work, first published by Dover Publications, Inc., in 2000.

DOVER *Pictorial Archive* SERIES

International Standard Book Number: 0-486-41039-0

Manufactured in the United States of America
Dover Publications, Inc., 31 East 2nd Street, Mineola, N.Y. 11501

NOTE

This book is designed to help children learn 250 French words while they enjoy coloring the drawings. The entire English alphabet is included. (Although the French alphabet does not include the letters *k* or *w,* some words from English and other languages that begin with those letters are used by French-speakers. Thus, all of the "French" words in this book that begin with *k* or *w* are spelled exactly or almost exactly like the word used in English for that object.)

Each page features one or two letters of the alphabet. Several drawings illustrate nouns and verbs that begin with each alphabet letter. In every case, the word in French appears below the matching illustration. To enable children to see both the French and the English word for each illustration, a French/English Word List has been provided at the back of the book.

In French, as in other languages based on Latin, nouns are divided by "gender" as masculine or feminine. For masculine nouns, "the" is indicated by *le.* For feminine nouns, "the" is indicated by *la.* The plural form is indicated by *les* for all nouns. When a noun begins with a vowel, or with a silent *h* followed by a vowel, the abbreviation *l'* is used before a singular noun to indicate "the" (*les* is used before plural nouns of this kind, however).

In this book, both below the illustrations and in the French/English Word List, when *l'* is used to indicate "the" before a noun, and when the plural form of a noun is used, the abbreviation (f.), for feminine, or (m.), for masculine, has been placed after the noun to identify its gender. (There is no single, simple rule for discovering the gender of a noun by its spelling or by other means. Knowing a noun's gender is necessary to form simple sentences, because adjectives such as "green," "small," and "lazy," and the indefinite articles—"a" and "an"— must match the noun's gender.)

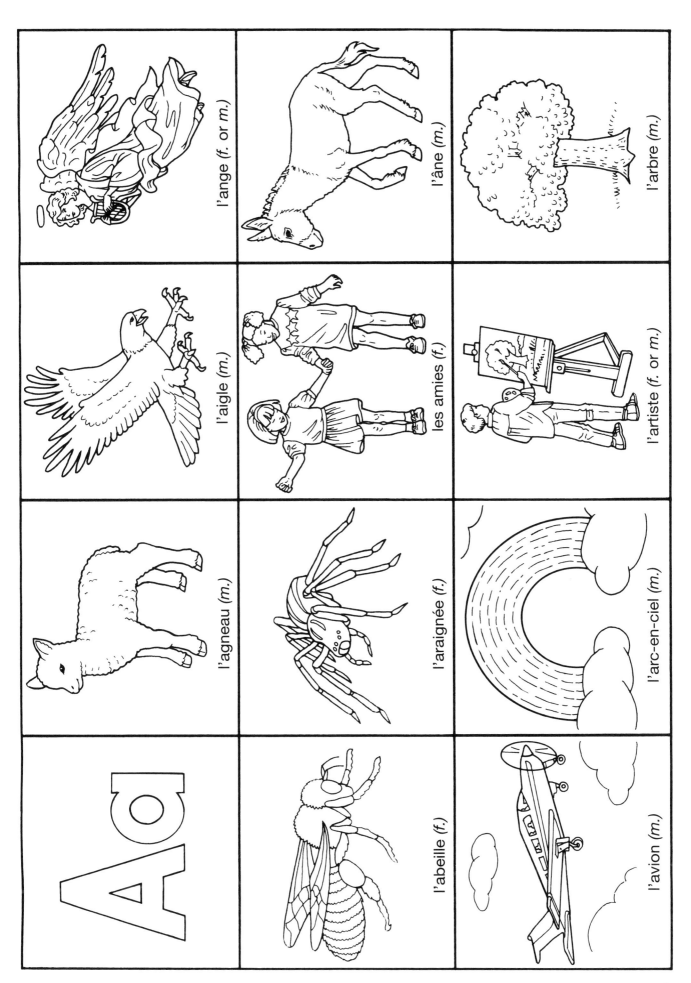

l'ange (f. or m.)

l'âne (m.)

l'arbre (m.)

l'aigle (m.)

les amies (f.)

l'artiste (f. or m.)

l'agneau (m.)

l'araignée (f.)

l'arc-en-ciel (m.)

l'abeille (f.)

l'avion (m.)

Aa

1

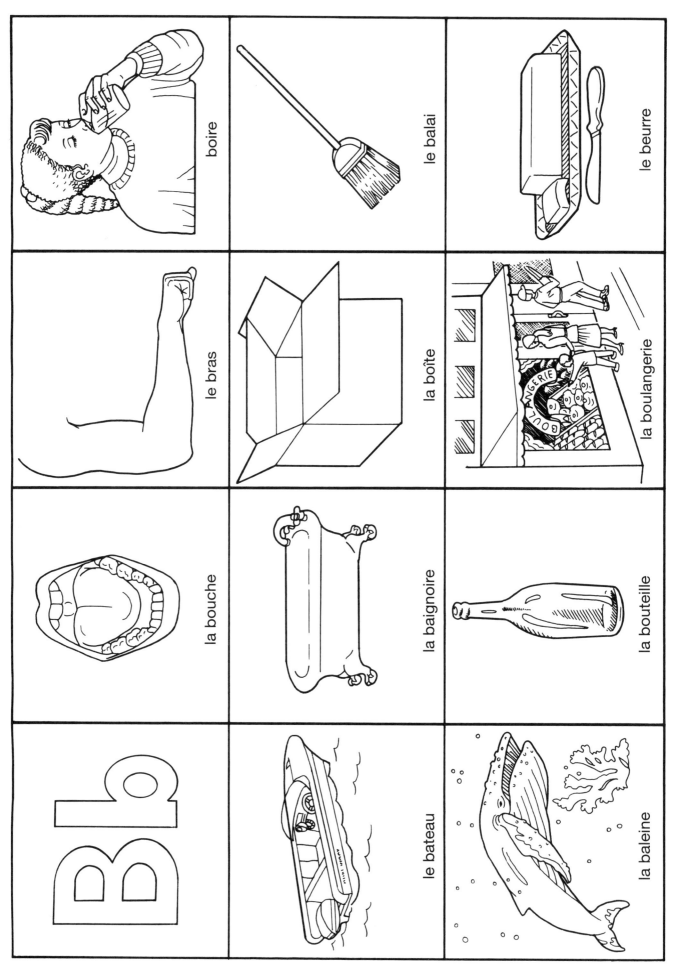

boire

le balai

le beurre

le bras

la boîte

la boulangerie

la bouche

la baignoire

la bouteille

Bb

le bateau

la baleine

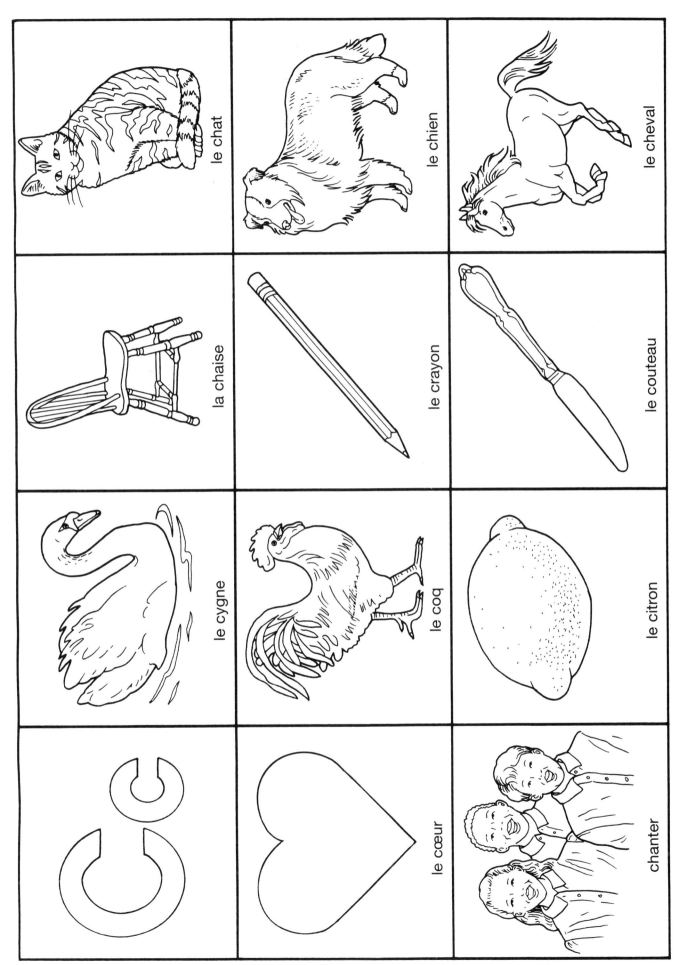

le chat

le chien

le cheval

la chaise

le crayon

le couteau

le cygne

le coq

le citron

le cœur

chanter

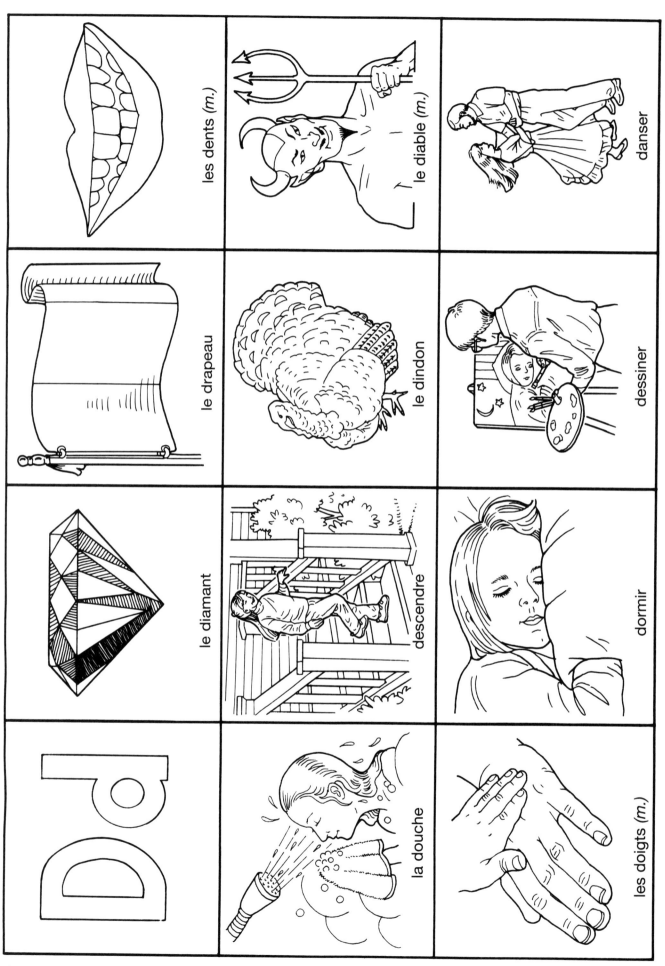

les dents (m.)

le diable (m.)

danser

le drapeau

le dindon

dessiner

le diamant

descendre

dormir

D d

la douche

les doigts (m.)

l'escalier (m.)

écouter

l'école (f.)

l'étoile (f.)

l'écureuil (m.)

écrire

l'échelle (f.)

l'éclair (m.)

l'enfant (m. or f.)

E e

les échecs (m.)

l'église (f.)

5

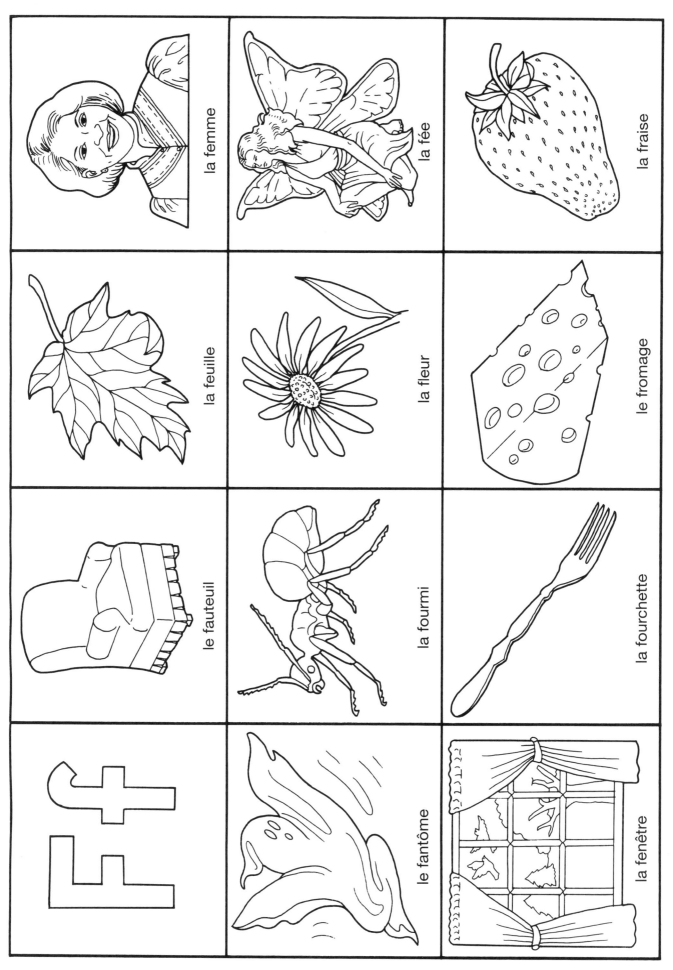

la femme

la fée

la fraise

la feuille

la fleur

le fromage

le fauteuil

la fourmi

la fourchette

le fantôme

la fenêtre

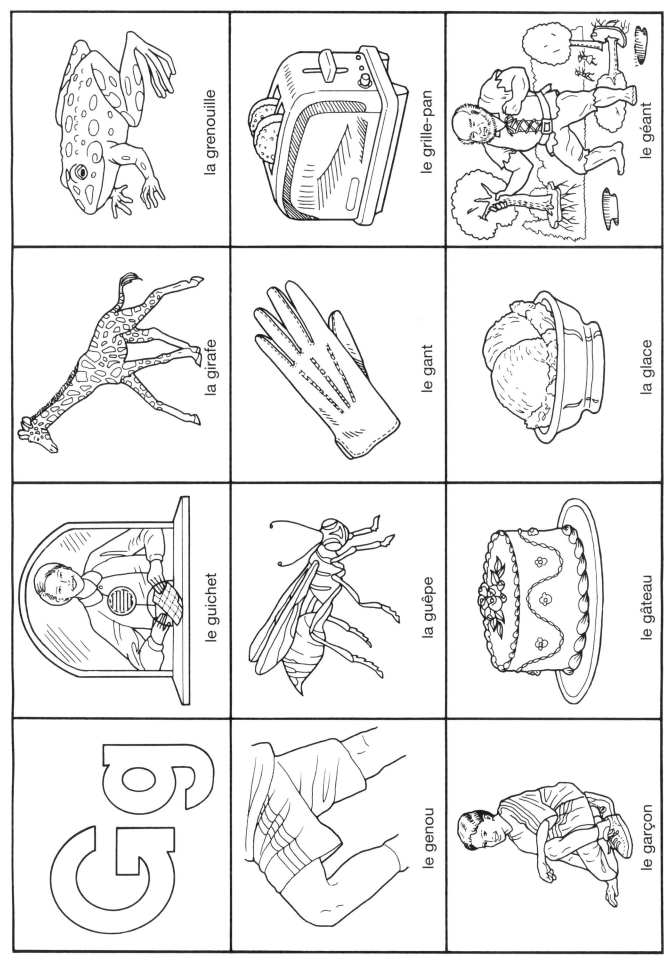

la grenouille

le grille-pan

le géant

la girafe

le gant

la glace

le guichet

la guêpe

le gâteau

Gg

le genou

le garçon

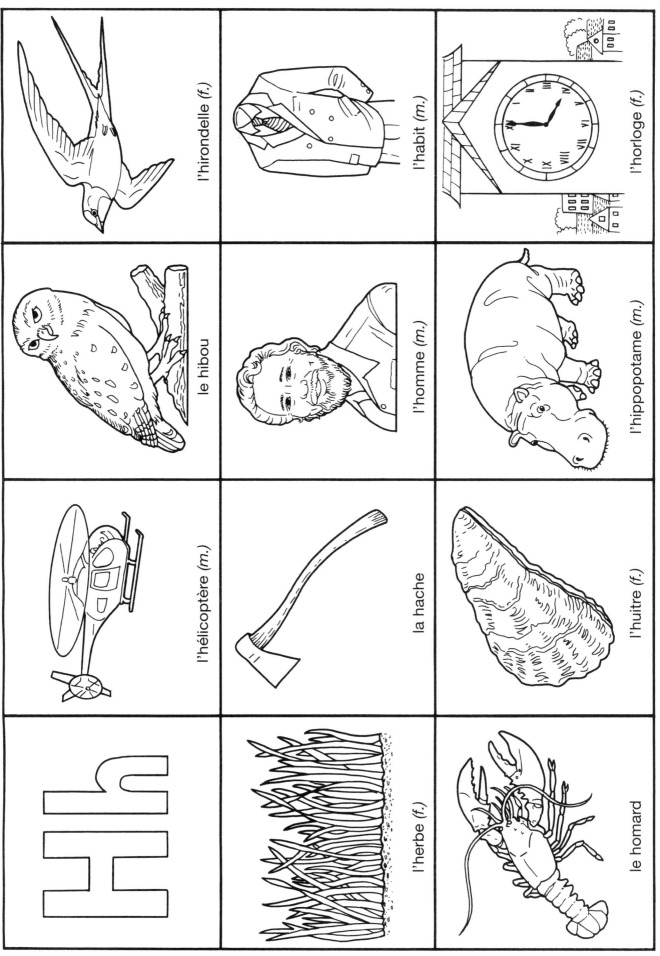

l'hirondelle (f.)

l'habit (m.)

l'horloge (f.)

le hibou

l'homme (m.)

l'hippopotame (m.)

l'hélicoptère (m.)

la hache

l'huitre (f.)

Hh

l'herbe (f.)

le homard

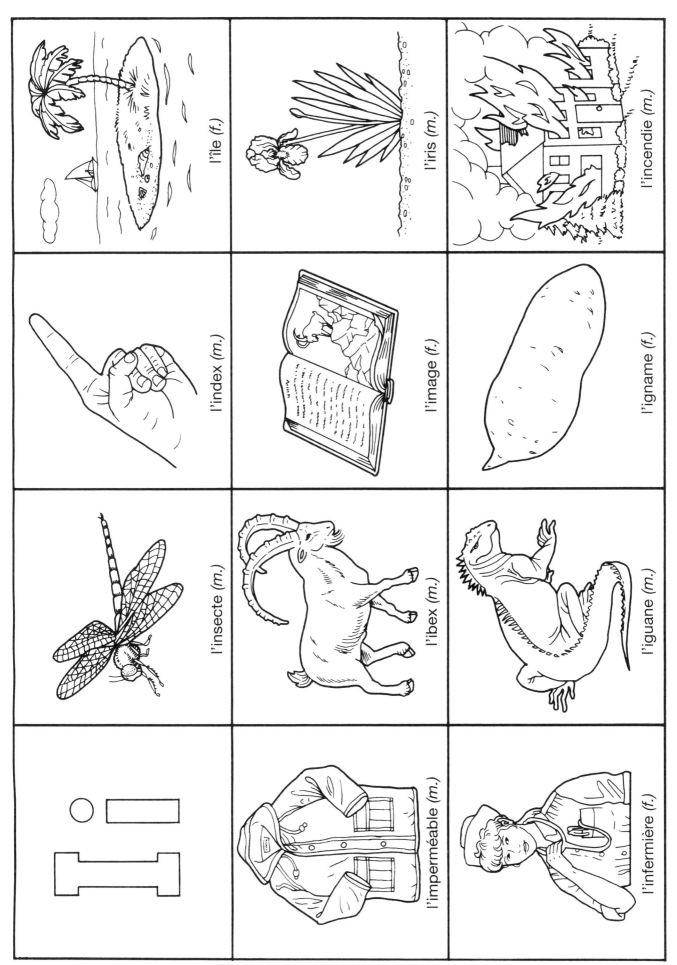

l'île (f.)

l'iris (m.)

l'incendie (m.)

l'index (m.)

l'image (f.)

l'igname (f.)

l'insecte (m.)

l'ibex (m.)

l'iguane (m.)

l'imperméable (m.)

l'infirmière (f.)

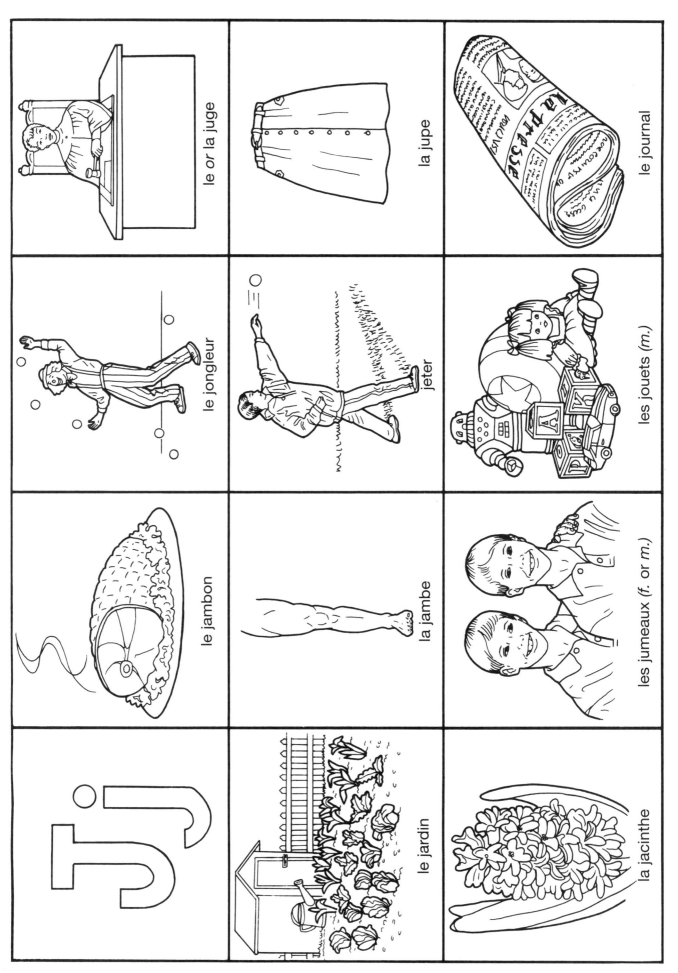

le or la juge

la jupe

le journal

le jongleur

jeter

les jouets (m.)

le jambon

la jambe

les jumeaux (f. or m.)

le jardin

la jacinthe

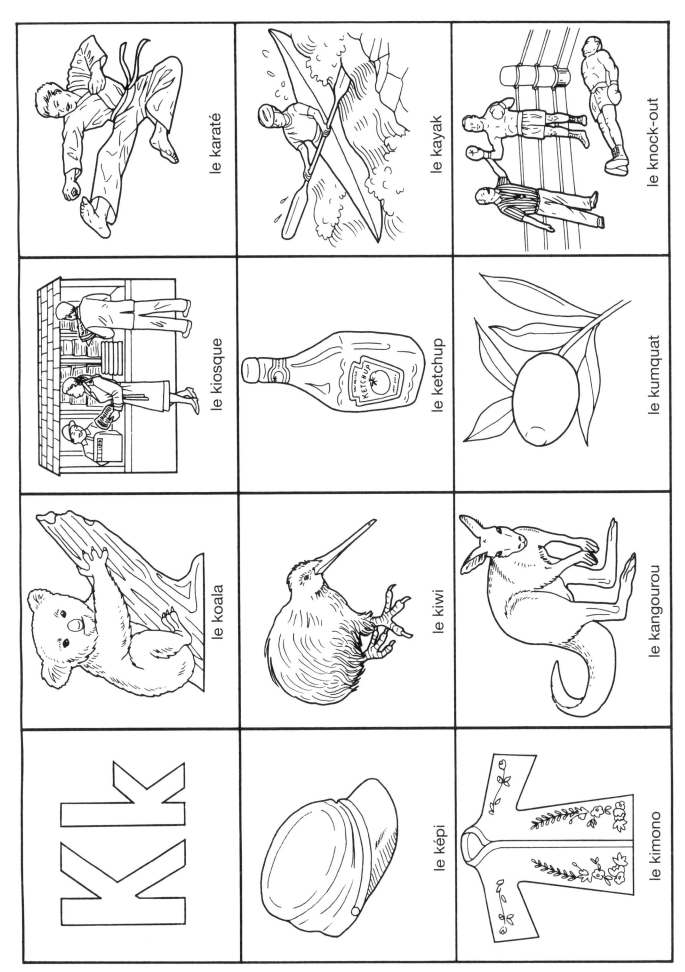

le karaté

le kayak

le knock-out

le kiosque

le ketchup

le kumquat

le koala

le kiwi

le kangourou

K k

le képi

le kimono

11

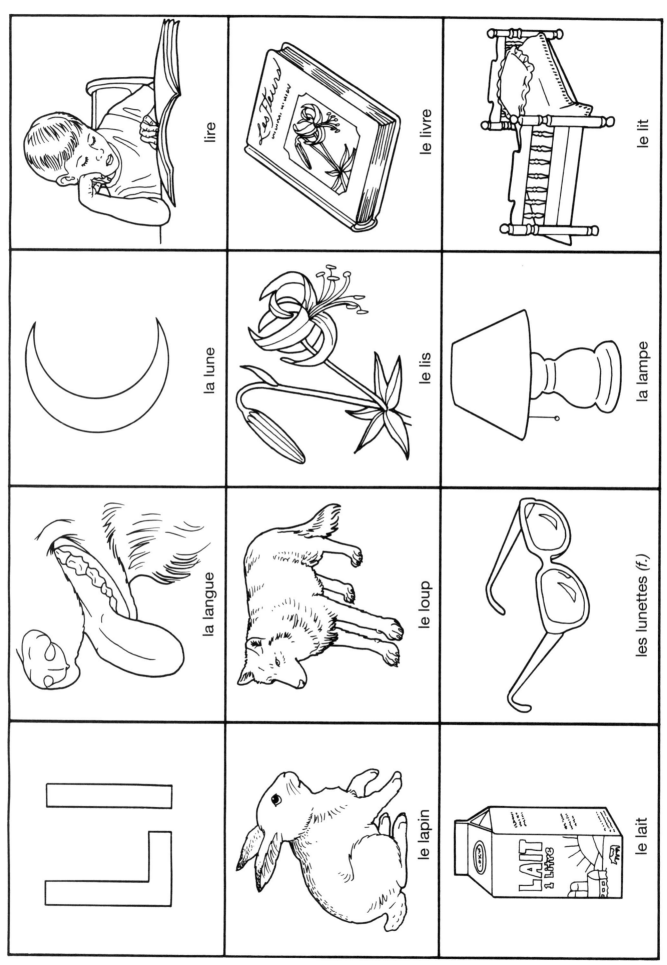

lire

le livre

le lit

la lune

le lis

la lampe

la langue

le loup

les lunettes (f.)

le lapin

le lait

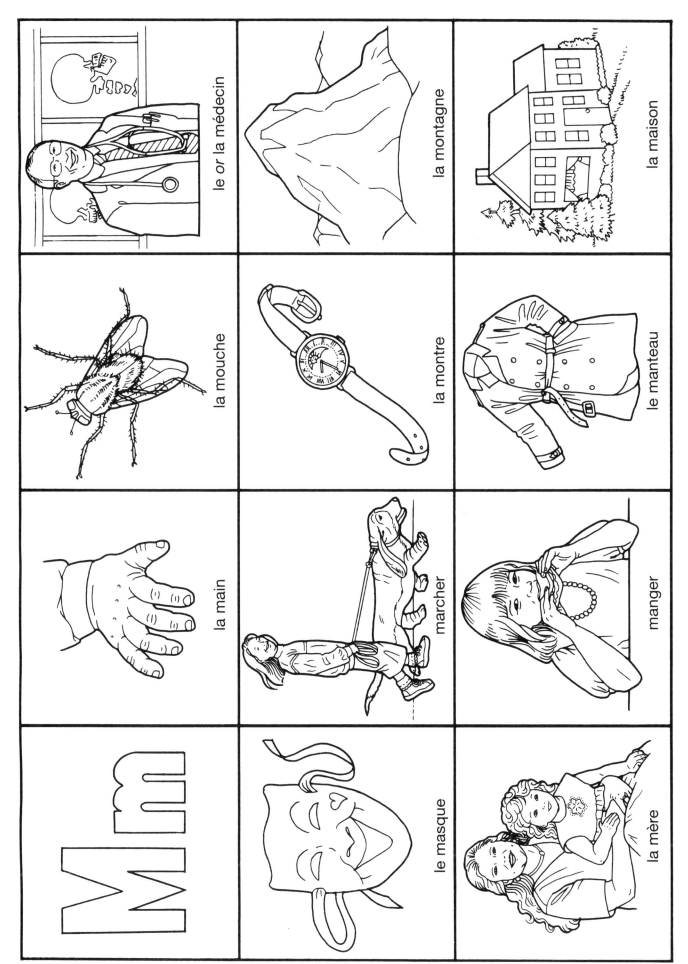

le or la médecin

la montagne

la maison

la mouche

la montre

le manteau

la main

marcher

manger

M m

le masque

la mère

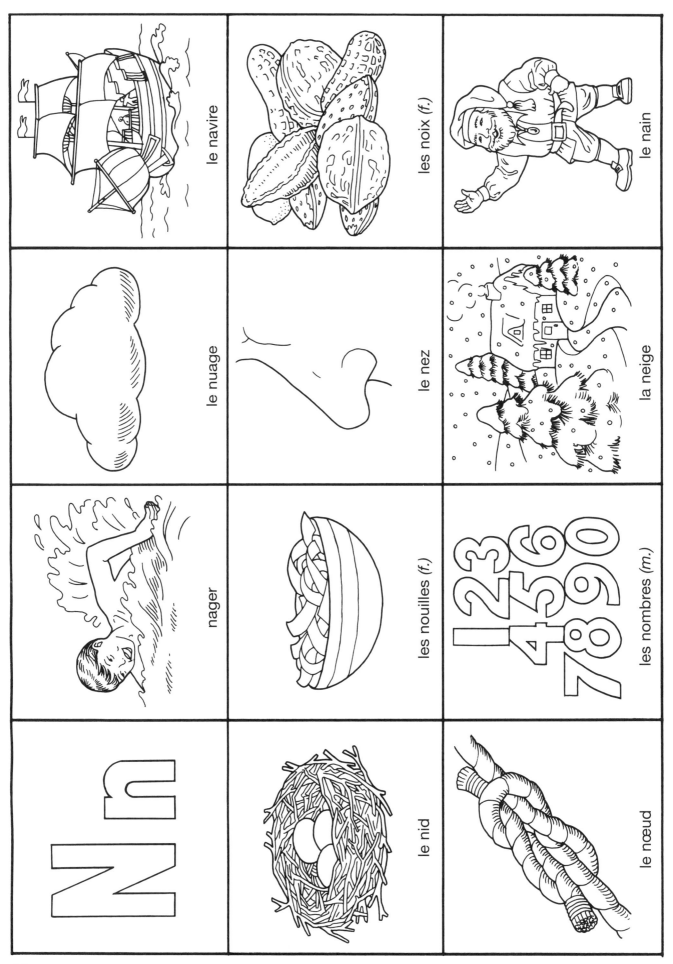

le navire

les noix (f.)

le nain

le nuage

le nez

la neige

nager

les nouilles (f.)

les nombres (m.)

N n

le nid

le nœud

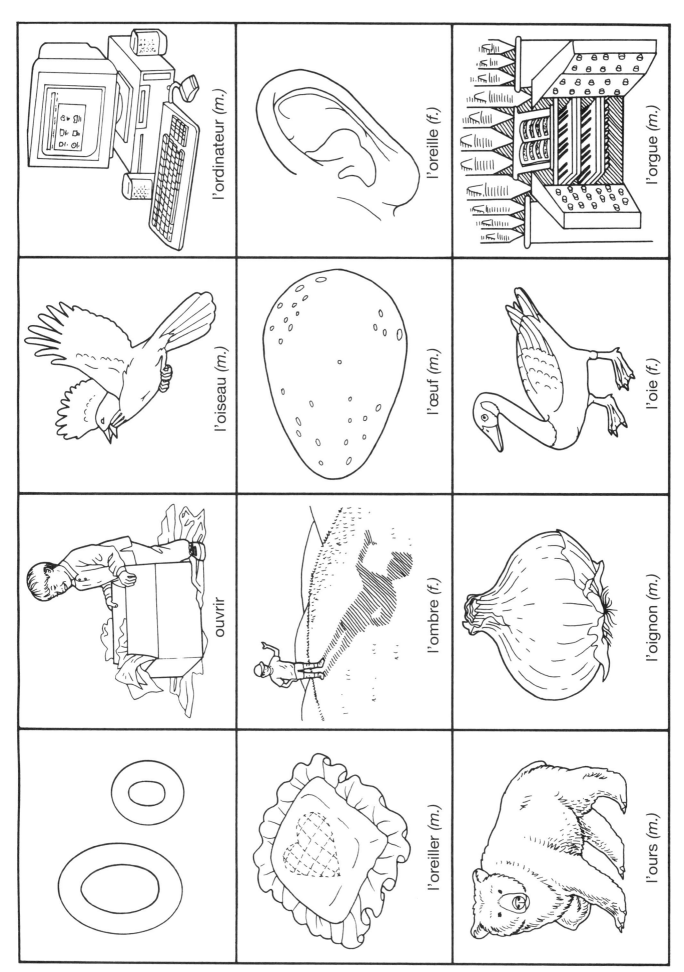

l'ordinateur (m.)

l'oreille (f.)

l'orgue (m.)

l'oiseau (m.)

l'œuf (m.)

l'oie (f.)

ouvrir

l'ombre (f.)

l'oignon (m.)

l'oreiller (m.)

l'ours (m.)

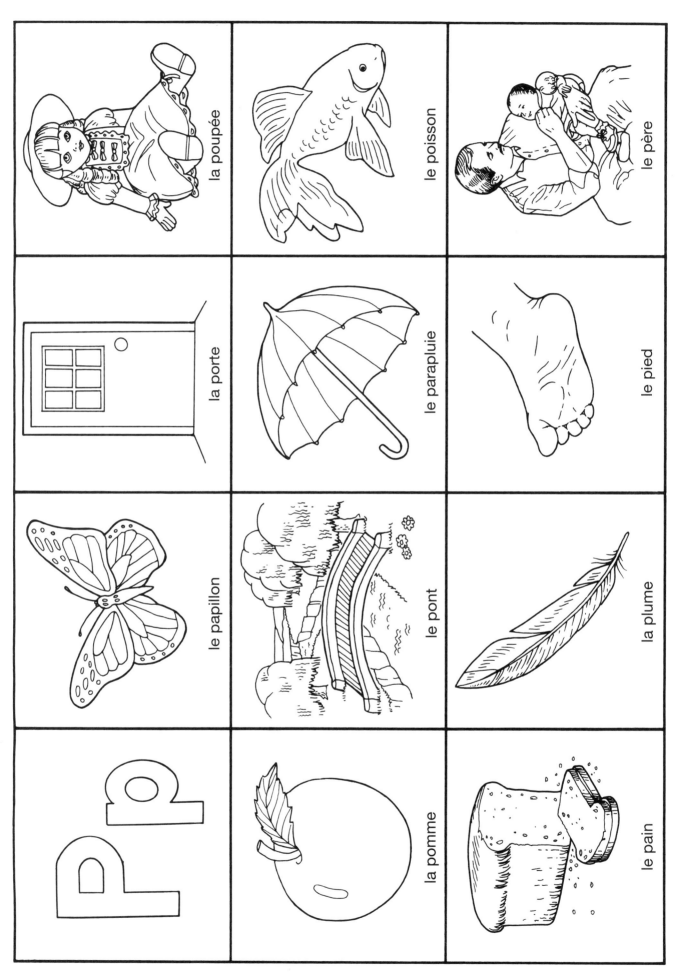

la poupée

le poisson

le père

la porte

le parapluie

le pied

le papillon

le pont

la plume

P p

la pomme

le pain

16

quarante

les quilles (f.)

le quatorze juillet

quatorze

la queue

quinze

quatre

le quai

quatre cent

le quartz

quatre-vingts

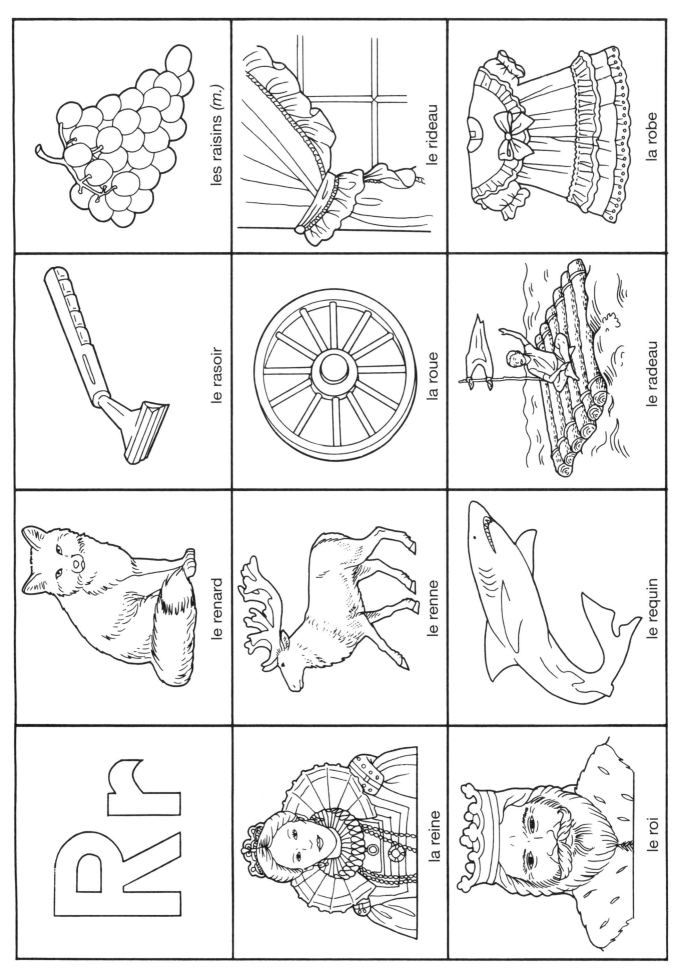

les raisins (m.)

le rideau

la robe

le rasoir

la roue

le radeau

le renard

le renne

le requin

Rr

la reine

le roi

18

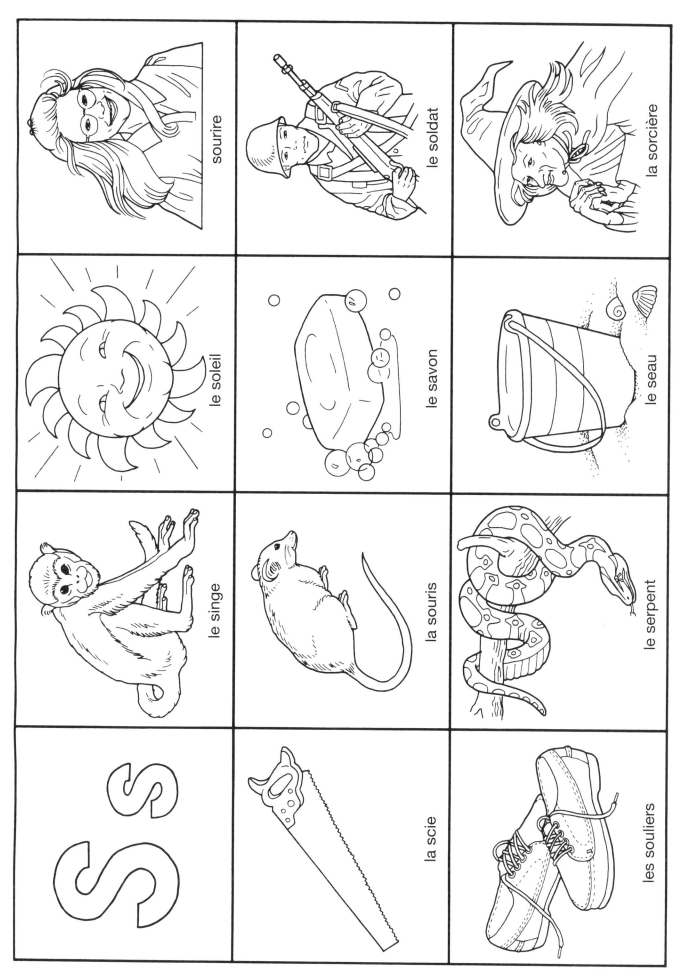

sourire

le soldat

la sorcière

le soleil

le savon

le seau

le singe

la souris

le serpent

S s

la scie

les souliers

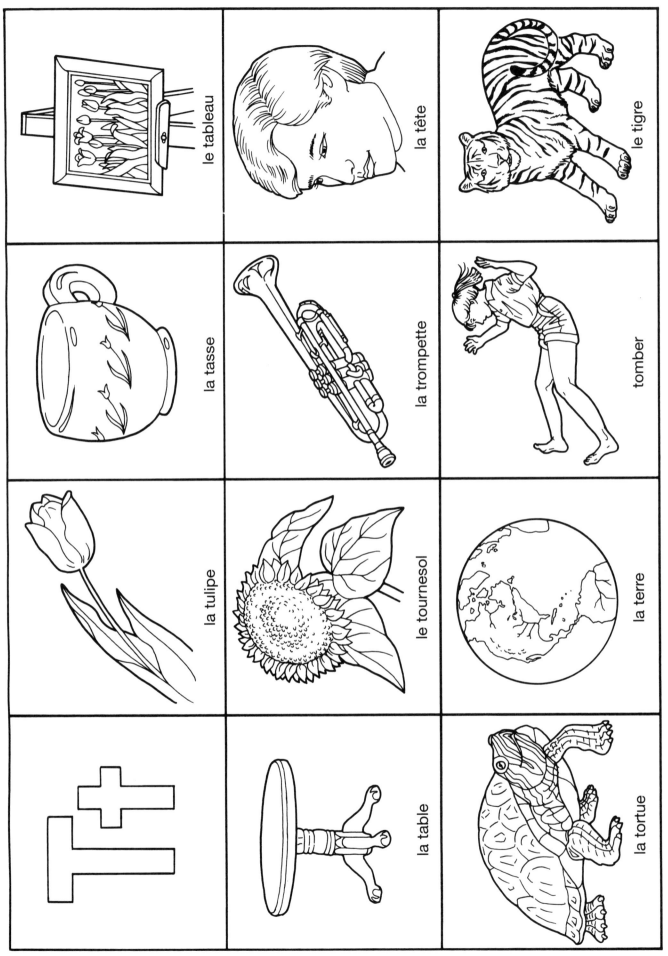

le tableau

la tête

le tigre

la tasse

la trompette

tomber

la tulipe

le tournesol

la terre

la table

la tortue

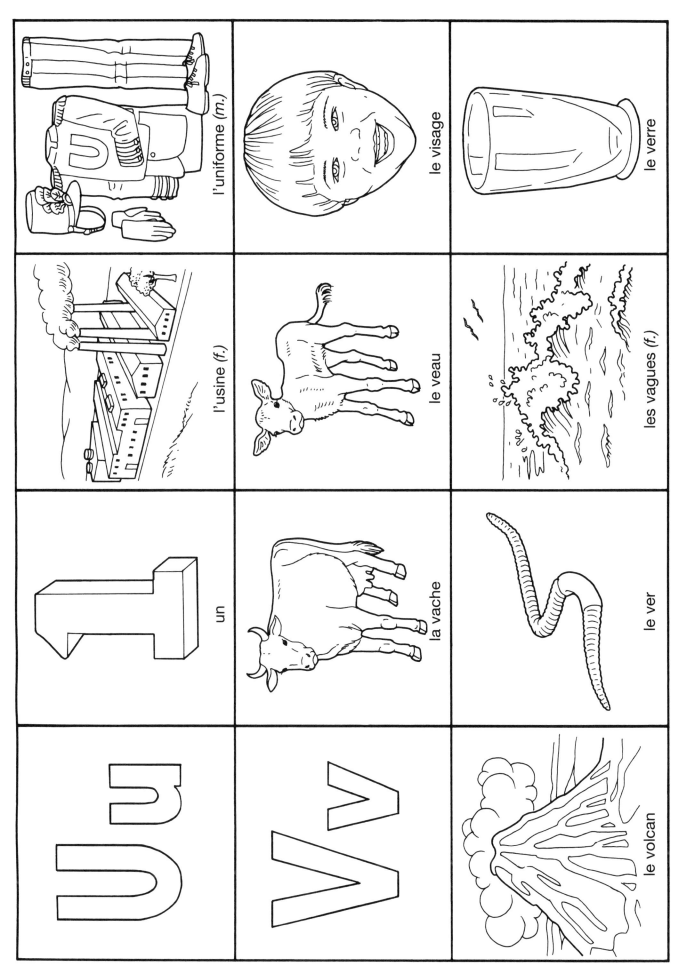

l'uniforme (m.)

le visage

le verre

l'usine (f.)

le veau

les vagues (f.)

un

la vache

le ver

U

V v

le volcan

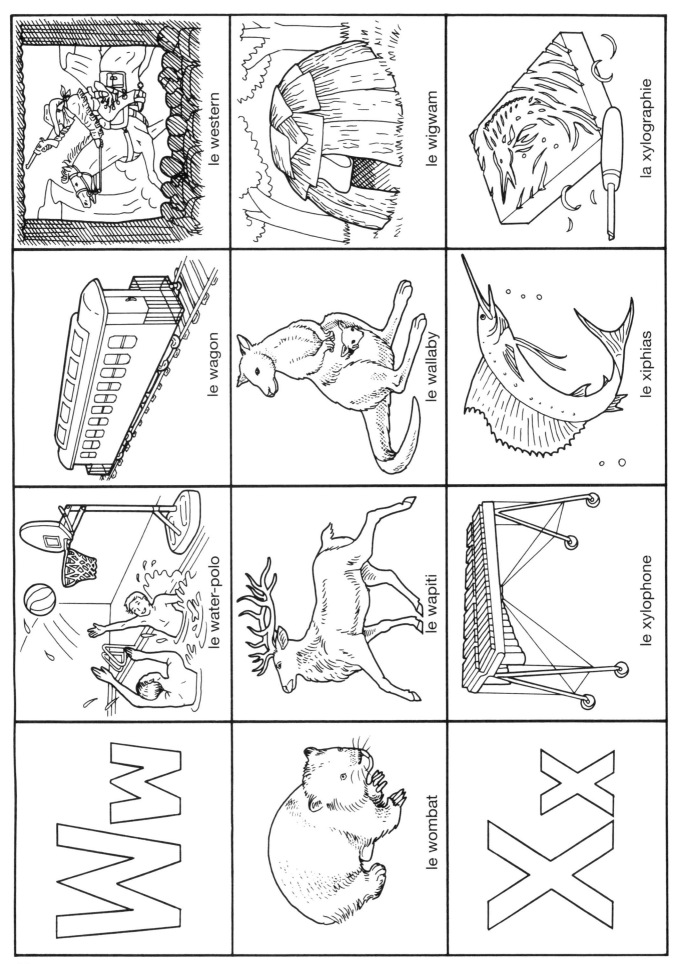

le western

le wigwam

la xylographie

le wagon

le wallaby

le xiphias

le water-polo

le wapiti

le xylophone

Ww

le wombat

Xx

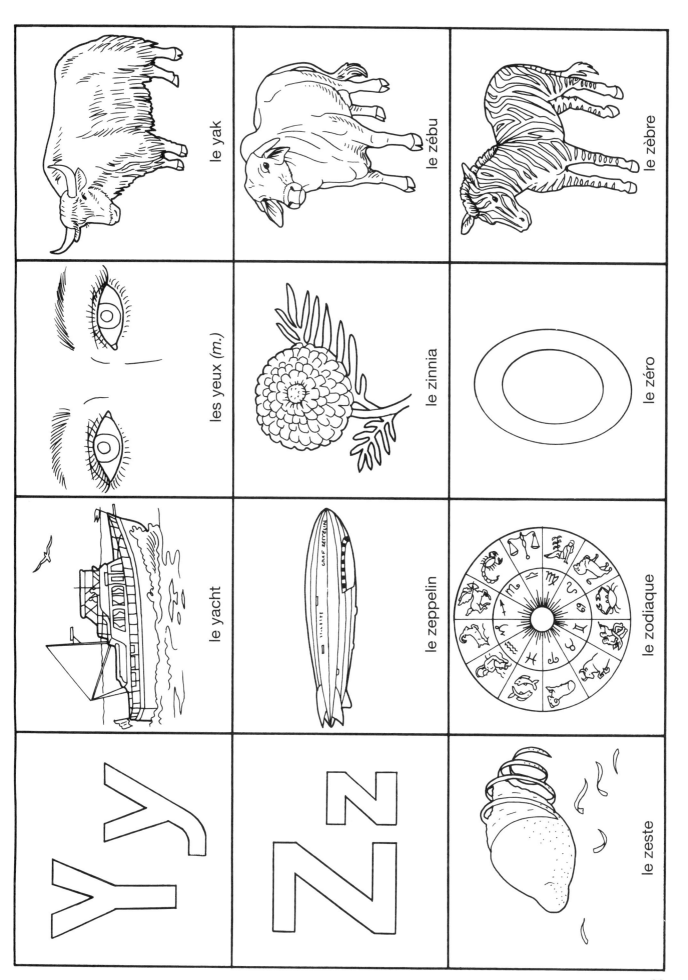

le yak

le zébu

le zèbre

les yeux (m.)

le zinnia

le zéro

le yacht

le zeppelin

le zodiaque

le zeste

23

FRENCH/ENGLISH WORD LIST

Page 1

l'abeille *(f.)* (bee)
l'agneau *(m.)* (lamb)
l'aigle *(m.)* (eagle)
les amies *(f.)* (friends)
l'âne *(m.)* (donkey)
l'ange *(m.* or *f.)* (angel)
l'araignée *(f.)* (spider)
l'arbre *(m.)* (tree)
l'arc-en-ciel *(m.)* (rainbow)
l'artiste *(m.* or *f.)* (artist)
l'avion *(m.)* (airplane)

Page 2

la baignoire (bathtub)
le balai (broom)
la baleine (whale)
le bateau (boat)
le beurre (butter)
boire (to drink)
la boîte (box)
la bouche (mouth)
la boulangerie (bakery)
la bouteille (bottle)
le bras (arm)

Page 3

la chaise (chair)
chanter (to sing)
le chat (cat)
le cheval (horse)
le chien (dog)
le citron (lemon)
le cœur (heart)
le coq (rooster)
le couteau (knife)
le crayon (pencil)
le cygne (swan)

Page 4

danser (to dance)
les dents *(m.)* (teeth)
descendre (to descend)
dessiner (to draw)
le diable (devil)
le diamant (diamond)
le dindon (turkey)
les doigts *(m.)* (fingers)
dormir (to sleep)
la douche (shower)
le drapeau (flag)

Page 5

les échecs *(m.)* (chess)
l'échelle *(f.)* (ladder)
l'éclair *(m.)* (lightning)
l'école *(f.)* (school)
écouter (to listen)
écrire (to write)
l'écureuil *(m.)* (squirrel)
l'église *(f.)* (church)
l'enfant *(m.* or *f.)* (child)
l'escalier *(m.)* (staircase)
l'étoile *(f.)* (star)

Page 6

le fantôme (ghost)
le fauteuil (armchair)
la fée (fairy)
la femme (woman)
la fenêtre (window)
la feuille (leaf)
la fleur (flower)
la fourchette (fork)
la fourmi (ant)
la fraise (strawberry)
le fromage (cheese)

Page 7

le gant (glove)
le garçon (boy)
le gâteau (cake)
le géant (giant)
le genou (knee)
la girafe (giraffe)
la glace (ice cream)
la grenouille (frog)
le grille-pan (toaster)
la guêpe (wasp)
le guichet (ticket window)

Page 8

l'habit (m.) (suit)
la hache (ax)
l'hélicoptère (m.) (helicopter)
l'herbe (f.) (grass)
le hibou (owl)
l'hippopotame (m.) (hippopotamus)
l'hirondelle (f.) (swallow)
le homard (lobster)
l'homme (m.) (man)
l'horloge (f.) (clock)
l'huitre (f.) (oyster)

Page 9

l'ibex (m.) (ibex)
l'igname (f.) (yam)
l'iguane (m.) (iguana)
l'île (f.) (island)
l'image (f.) (picture)
l'imperméable (m.) (raincoat)
l'incendie (m.) (fire)
l'index (m.) (index finger)
l'infirmière (f.) (nurse)
l'insecte (m.) (insect)
l'iris (m.) (iris)

Page 10

la jacinthe (hyacinth)
la jambe (leg)
le jambon (ham)
le jardin (garden)
jeter (to throw)

le jongleur (juggler)
les jouets (m.) (toys)
le journal (newspaper)
la or le juge (judge)
les jumeaux (m. or f.) (twins)
la jupe (skirt)

Page 11

le kangourou (kangaroo)
le karaté (karate)
le kayak (kayak)
le képi (cap)
le ketchup (ketchup)
le kimono (kimono)
le kiosque (kiosk)
le kiwi (kiwi)
le knock-out (knockout)
le koala (koala)
le kumquat (kumquat)

Page 12

le lait (milk)
la lampe (lamp)
la langue (tongue)
le lapin (rabbit)
lire (to read)
le lis (lily)
le lit (bed)
le livre (book)
le loup (wolf)
la lune (moon)
les lunettes (f.) (eyeglasses)

Page 13

la main (hand)
la maison (house)
manger (to eat)
le manteau (coat)
marcher (to walk)
le masque (mask)
le or la médecin (doctor)
la mère (mother)
la montagne (mountain)
la montre (watch)
la mouche (fly)

Page 14

nager (to swim)
le nain (dwarf)
le navire (ship)
la neige (snow)
le nez (nose)
le nid (nest)
le nœud (knot)
les noix *(f.)* (nuts)
les nombres *(m.)* (numbers)
les nouilles *(f.)* (noodles)
le nuage (cloud)

Page 15

l'œuf *(m.)* (egg)
l'oie *(f.)* (goose)
l'oignon *(m.)* (onion)
l'oiseau *(m.)* (bird)
l'ombre *(f.)* (shadow)
l'ordinateur *(m.)* (computer)
l'oreille *(f.)* (ear)
l'oreiller *(m.)* (pillow)
l'orgue *(m.)* (organ)
l'ours *(m.)* (bear)
ouvrir (to open)

Page 16

le pain (bread)
le papillon (butterfly)
le parapluie (umbrella)
le père (father)
le pied (foot)
la plume (feather; also used for pen)
le poisson (fish)
la pomme (apple)
le pont (bridge)
la porte (door)
la poupée (doll)

Page 17

le quai (dock)
quarante (forty)
le quartz (quartz)
quatorze (fourteen)

le quatorze juillet (July 14—
    Bastille Day holiday)
quatre (four)
quatre cent (four hundred)
quatre-vingts (eighty)
la queue (tail)
les quilles *(f.)* (ninepins)
quinze (fifteen)

Page 18

le radeau (raft)
les raisins *(m.)* (grapes)
le rasoir (razor)
la reine (queen)
le renard (fox)
le renne (reindeer)
le requin (shark)
le rideau (curtain)
la robe (dress)
le roi (king)
la roue (wheel)

Page 19

le savon (soap)
la scie (saw)
le seau (pail)
le serpent (snake)
le singe (monkey)
le soldat (soldier)
le soleil (sun)
la sorcière (witch)
les souliers (shoes)
sourire (to smile)
la souris (mouse)

Page 20

la table (table)
le tableau (painting)
la tasse (cup)
la terre (Earth)
la tête (head)
le tigre (tiger)
tomber (to fall)
la tortue (turtle)
le tournesol (sunflower)
la trompette (trumpet)
la tulipe (tulip)

Page 21

un (one)
l'uniforme *(m.)* (uniform)
l'usine *(f.)* (factory)
la vache (cow)
les vagues *(f.)* (waves)
le veau (calf)
le ver (worm)
le verre (glass)
le visage (face)
le volcan (volcano)

Page 22

le wagon (railroad car)
le wallaby (wallaby)
le wapiti (wapiti)
le water-polo (water polo)

le western (Western film)
le wigwam (wigwam)
le wombat (wombat)
le xiphias (swordfish)
la xylographie (woodcut)
le xylophone (xylophone)

Page 23

le yacht (yacht)
le yak (yak)
les yeux *(m.)* (eyes)
le zèbre (zebra)
le zébu (zebu)
le zeppelin (zeppelin)
le zéro (zero)
le zeste (citrus fruit peel)
le zinnia (zinnia)
le zodiaque (zodiac)